FROM THE FILMS OF

Harry Potter

CREATE BY STICKER: HOGSMEADE

SCHOLASTIC INC.

WIZARDING WORLD

ISBN 978-1-338-71597-2

10 9 8 7 6 5 4 3 2 1   21 22 23 24 25
Printed in Malaysia   106

First edition 2021

By Cala Spinner
Book design by Jessica Meltzer
Interior illustrations by Artful Doodlers

"Remember: These visits to Hogsmeade Village are a privilege."

—Professor McGonagall, *Harry Potter and the Prisoner of Azkaban*

Beginning in their third year, Hogwarts students are permitted to visit **Hogsmeade**, an all-wizarding village situated on the outskirts of the castle. From the onset, Hogsmeade teems with magic— from the stunning snowcapped buildings to the nefarious **Zonko's Joke Shop**; from the delightful **Three Broomsticks** to the not-so-delightful **Hog's Head Inn**. Everything is magical and a sight to behold.

Of course, entering Hogsmeade is a privilege. Students without their guardians' signature are not permitted to visit . . . like poor Harry, who, in the third film, can't convince Uncle Vernon to sign his form before magicking his aunt away.

For those *allowed* to enter Hogsmeade, there's lots to see and do. In this book, you'll help finish the images and scenes of the enchanting village by matching the numbered stickers in the back to the numbers on the page.

When you're done, the image will be complete. Then you can turn the page and complete the next one, and the next one, and the next!

When Fred and George Weasley learn that Harry can't visit Hogsmeade, they gift him the **Marauder's Map**. It's an enchanted, magical map that reveals **secret passageways** in and out of Hogwarts, as well as the names of all who inhabit the grounds (and where they are at any given moment, should Harry be on the lookout for a certain Severus Snape).

Harry uses the Marauder's Map to sneak into Hogsmeade. Use your stickers on page 25 to complete the image!

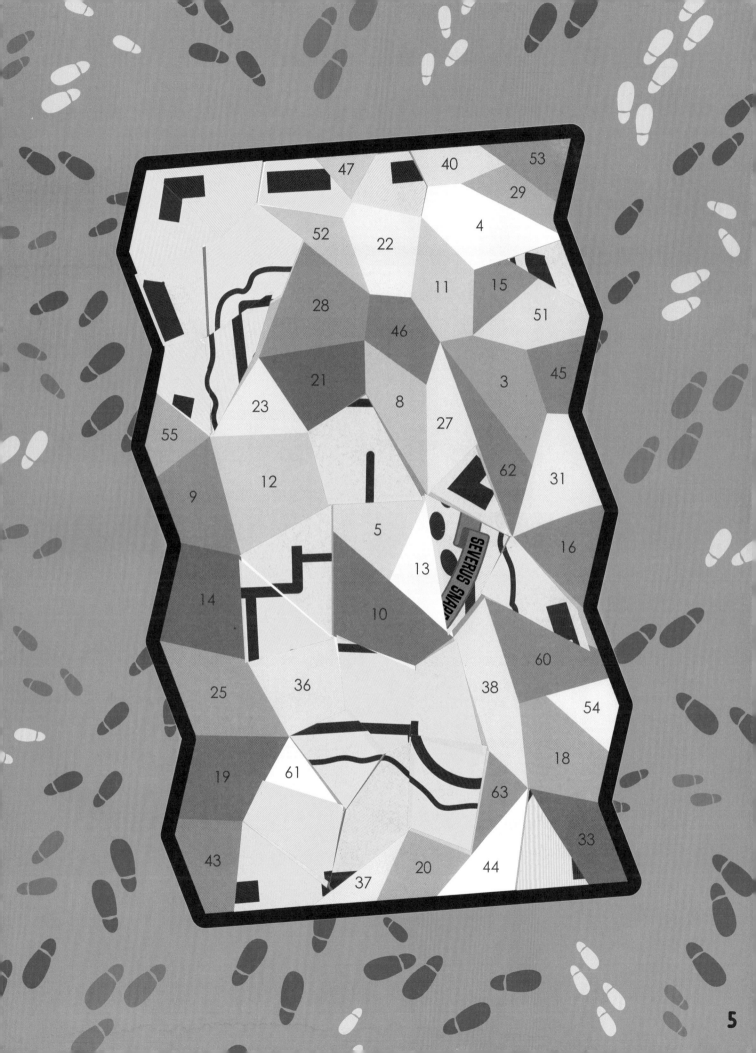

In their first visit to Hogsmeade, Hermione and Ron have a run-in with none other than **Draco Malfoy**. Malfoy taunts the twosome by calling them names. But before he can finish, he gets pummeled by a rogue **snowball**.

Use your stickers on page 27 to reveal who threw the snowball. Could it be someone hiding underneath the **Invisibility Cloak**?

Hogsmeade is home to many shops and businesses. One of their most popular locales is **Honeydukes**—a delicious, tasty shop brimming with treats, sweets, and more! There's **Bertie Bott's Every Flavor Beans**, **Chocolate Frogs**, **Fizzing Whizzbees**, **Peppermint Toads**, and **Cauldron Cakes**, just to name a few. Even Professor Umbridge's too-sugary tea can't compete with what's in store.

One Hogwarts student in particular really loves Acid Pops. Use your stickers on page 29 to discover who!

Of course, no trip to Hogsmeade is complete without visiting **Zonko's Joke Shop**. Zonko's carries **tricks** and **pranks** that could satisfy even Fred and George Weasley. Some of their products include Dungbombs and sugar quills, which are somehow equally good for both snacking and taking tests.

Use your stickers on page 31 to reveal what Ginny buys from Zonko's.

Gladrags Wizardwear is another shop inside Hogsmeade where witches and wizards can purchase robes, socks, and other fine clothing.

Use your stickers on page 33 to reveal what Hermione, Viktor Krum, Ron, and Parvati wore to the Yule Ball.

POST OFFICE ·OWL POST·

Hogsmeade is home to its own **post office** too, which houses **owls** of all kinds that transport mail to and from the village.

Use your stickers on page 35 to complete the image of Cho at the post office.

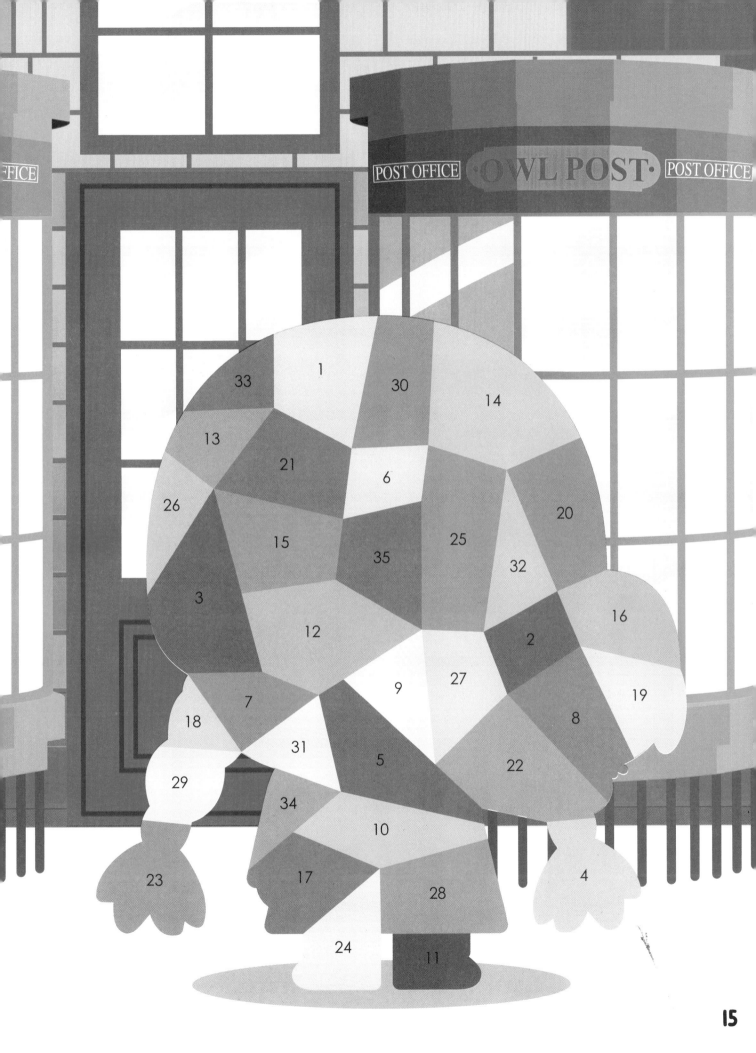

Located a few streets away from the hustle and bustle of Hogsmeade proper is the **Hog's Head Inn**. In the fifth film, Harry hosts the first meeting of Dumbledore's Army at the pub, and eventually uses it as a **secret entrance** to the castle during the Battle of Hogwarts. Who owns the Hog's Head Inn?

Use your stickers on page 37 to reveal the answer on the next page.

Also off the beaten path is the **Shrieking Shack**. It's an abandoned house that's rumored to be crawling with ghosts and the like. However, little do most Hogsmeade dwellers know, the Shrieking Shack is actually a **secret entrance** to Hogwarts—and it was constructed for a student who turned into a **werewolf** every full moon.

Who was the Shrieking Shack made for? Use your stickers on page 39 to discover the answer!

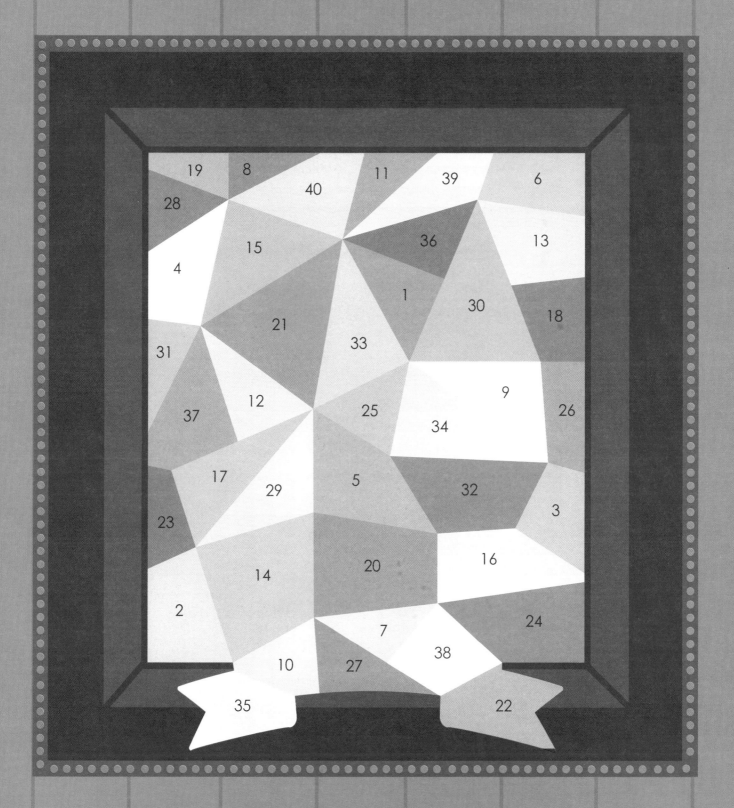

Perhaps the most frequented locale in all of Hogsmeade is the **Three Broomsticks Inn** — a gorgeous, popular pub that's run by a witch named **Madam Rosmerta**. Here, patrons can order drinks while enjoying one another's company.

Harry, Ron, and Hermione shared many important moments at the Three Broomsticks in the films. Use your stickers on page 41 to reveal what their favorite order was.

Hogsmeade is a very special town, filled with **gorgeous scenery**, amazing shops, and wonderful treats. But perhaps most iconic to Hogsmeade is what it all looks like together — **snowcapped** buildings and all!

Use your stickers on page 43 to complete the image of Hogsmeade Village.

JOKES TRICKS ZON

25

27

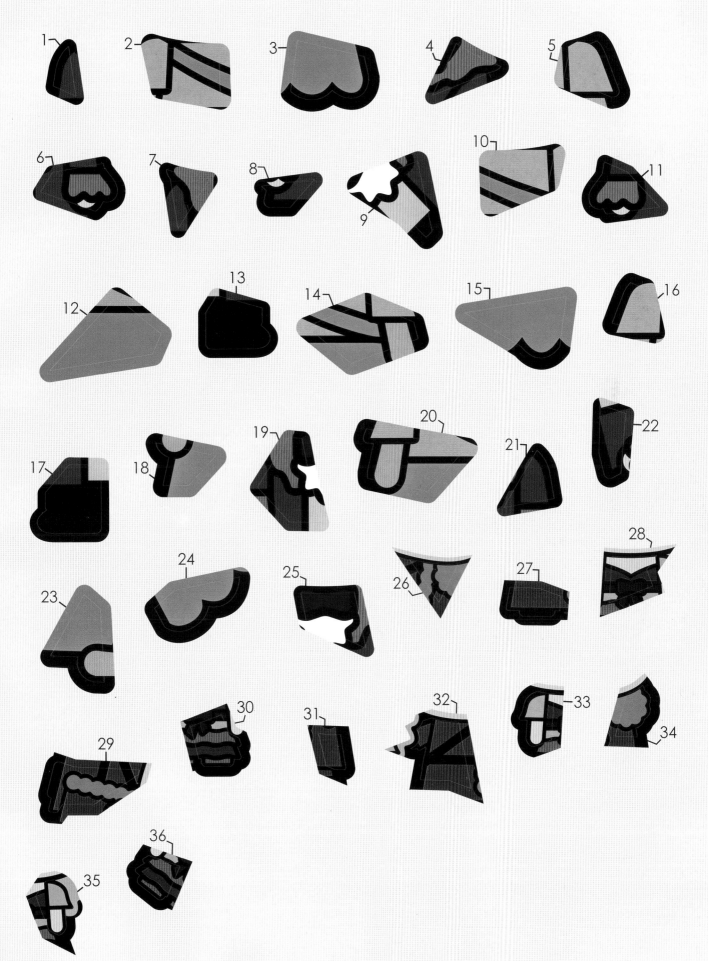

35

43